One I Love, Two I Love

One I Love, Two I Love

AND OTHER LOVING MOTHER GOOSE RHYMES

ILLUSTRATED BY
NONNY HOGROGIAN

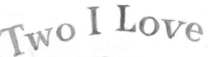

19762

E. P. DUTTON & CO., INC. NEW YORK

Illustrations copyright © 1972 by Nonny Hogrogian. All rights reserved.
Published simultaneously in Canada by Clarke, Irwin & Company Limited.
SBN: 0-525-36420-x · LCC: 79-179047   Printed in the U.S.A.   First Edition

One I love,
Two I love,
Three I love, I say;
Four I love with all my heart,
Five I cast away;
Six he loves me,
Seven he don't,
Eight we're lovers both;
Nine he comes,
Ten he tarries,
Eleven he courts,
Twelve he marries.

Peter, Peter, pumpkin eater,
Had a wife and couldn't keep her;
He put her in a pumpkin shell,
And there he kept her very well.

On Saturday night I lost my wife,
And where do you think I found her?
Up in the moon, singing a tune,
And all the stars around her.

Curly locks, curly locks,
    Wilt thou be mine?
Thou shalt not wash dishes
    Nor yet feed the swine;
But sit on a cushion
    And sew a fine seam,
And feed upon strawberries,
    Sugar and cream.

Old woman, old woman,
　Shall we go a-shearing?
Speak a little louder, sir,
　I'm very thick of hearing.
Old woman, old woman,
　Shall I love you dearly?
Thank you very kindly, sir,
　Now I hear you clearly.

Daffy-down-dilly is new come to town,
With a yellow petticoat, and a green gown.

Oh, rare Harry Parry,
When will you marry?
When apples and pears are ripe.
I'll come to your wedding
Without any bidding,
And dance and sing all the night.

Willy, Willy Wilkin,
Kissed the maids a-milking,
    Fa, la, la!
And with his merry daffing,
He set them all a-laughing,
    Ha, ha, ha!

Wine and cakes for gentlemen,
  Hay and corn for horses,
A cup of ale for good old wives,
  And kisses for young lasses.

Sukey, you shall be my wife
   And I will tell you why:
I have got a little pig,
   And you have got a sty;
I have got a dun cow,
   And you can make good cheese;
Sukey, will you marry me?
   Say Yes, if you please.

Doodledy, doodledy, doodledy, dan,
I'll have the piper to be my good-man;
And if I get less meat, I shall have game,
Doodledy, doodledy, doodledy, dan.

Scissors and string, scissors and string,
When a man's single he lives like a king.
Needles and pins, needles and pins,
When a man marries his trouble begins.

Whistle, daughter, whistle,
  And you shall have a sheep.
Mother, I cannot whistle,
  Neither can I sleep.

Whistle, daughter, whistle,
  And you shall have a cow.
Mother, I cannot whistle,
  Neither know I how.

Whistle, daughter, whistle,
  And you shall have a man.
Mother, I cannot whistle,
  But I'll do the best I can.

Georgie Porgie, pudding and pie,
Kissed the girls and made them cry;
When the boys came out to play,
Georgie Porgie ran away.

Ickle ockle, blue bockle,
Fishes in the sea,
If you want a pretty maid
Please choose me.

Terence McDiddler,
   The three-stringed fiddler,
Can charm, if you please,
   The fish from the seas.

Good morrow to you, Valentine.
Curl your locks as I do mine,
Two before and three behind.
Good morrow to you, Valentine.